No Difference Between Us

by Jayneen Sanders

illustrated by Amanda Gulliver

Teaching children about gender equality, respectful relationships, feelings, choice, self-esteem, empathy, tolerance, and acceptance

D0701893

Dedication

For children everywhere.
Stand tall, stand strong,
stand proud.
You are amazing!

JS

"We're all people with feelings, aspirations and
dreams... no better or worse... it's the little
differences that make us unique but it doesn't
change the big ways that we are the same."

Susannah Low
Designer and mother of two daughters

No Difference Between Us
Educate2Empower Publishing an imprint of
UpLoad Publishing Pty Ltd
Victoria Australia
www.upload.com.au

First published in 2016

Text copyright © Jayneen Sanders 2016
Illustration copyright © Amanda Gulliver 2016

Written by Jayneen Sanders
Illustrations by Amanda Gulliver

Designed by Susannah Low, Butterflyrocket Design

All rights reserved. No part of this publication may be reproduced,
stored in a retrieval system, or transmitted in any way or by any means,
electronic, mechanical, photocopying, recording or otherwise, without
the prior written permission of UpLoad Publishing Pty Ltd.

Printed in China through Book Production Solutions

National Library of Australia
Cataloguing-in-Publication Data

Creator: Sanders, Jayneen, author.

Title: No difference between us:
teaching children about gender equality, respectful relationships,
feelings, choice, self-esteem, empathy, tolerance, and acceptance /
by Jayneen Sanders; illustrated by Amanda Gulliver.

ISBN: 9781925089271 (paperback)

Target Audience: For primary school age.

Subjects: Equality--Juvenile fiction.
Similarity (Psychology)--Juvenile fiction.
Siblings--Juvenile fiction.

Other Creators/Contributors: Gulliver, Amanda, illustrator.

Dewey Number: A823.4

Note to the Reader

The purpose of this book is to encourage equality and respect for each other from the earliest of years. In order to reduce gender-based violence we need to teach gender equality and respectful relationships to young children. What better way than through a picture storybook? Children are visual learners and the match between illustration and text in this story will assist them to understand that we are all human — everyone feels, and everyone has hopes and dreams. Our gender should be and needs to be irrelevant.

Throughout the text, open-ended questions are provided on each spread so children have the opportunity to talk about their own experiences — allowing the child to have a voice. There are more in-depth Discussion Questions on pages 30 and 31 encouraging the reader and the child to think about each scenario, and engage with the message.

I hope the children you read this story to both enjoy it, and embrace its message of equality and respect. This book can be read with children as young as three years old.

 My sister and I are different in **tiny little** ways.

Jess has oatmeal for breakfast, but...

I love eggs on toast!

4

? What do you like to have for breakfast?

Ben has short brown hair that sticks up in the air, but...

I have long straight hair that flips and flies when I run.

What kind of hair do you have?

Jess likes to play her guitar as loudly as she can, but...

I like to sing with my friends in the school choir.

 I like climbing trees way up to the top, but...

Ben is happy on the ground playing in the sand.

? *What kinds of things do you like to do?*

My sister and I are different
in **tiny little** ways, but...

sometimes we are EXACTLY the same.

Sometimes, there is NO difference between us!

Ben likes to play soccer on Saturday afternoons, and so do I.

Ben is a fast runner, just like me.

Ben likes hiking, and I do too.

12

? What sports or outdoor activities do you like to do?

When it's raining and we have to stay inside, Jess likes to play doctors, and so do I!

Jess checks the dolls with her stethoscope and carefully feels their heads.

When Jess is done, I gently wrap each doll up one by one and place them in their beds.

Sometimes Jess has to operate and I always help.

? What kinds of things do you like to play when you stay inside?

When we grow up, Ben and I want to be different things.

Ben wants to be a singer or drive a big machine.

I want to be a doctor or play my guitar in a rock-and-roll band.

? What do you think you might
like to be when you grow up?

When Jess is older she wants a family of her own, and so do I!

Jess wants two kids, one dog, and a cat called Kippers.

I want four kids, two rabbits, and a canary that sings.

? What might your family be like when you are grown up?

My brother and I are different in **tiny little** ways, but...

we are the same in so many other ways too.

Jess likes to cook cakes and I like to cook pancakes.

But we BOTH like cooking.

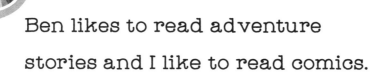

Ben likes to read adventure stories and I like to read comics.

But we BOTH like reading.

Jess likes to swim in the sea and I like to swim in a pool.

But we BOTH like swimming.

? How are you different in tiny little ways from your sister or brother or friend?

How are you exactly the same?

Ben feels scared when a storm is near, and so do I.

Jess feels sad when someone is hurt, and I do too.

Ben feels happy and safe tucked up in bed, just like me!

happy

sad

worried

scared

Sometimes I feel happy and sometimes I feel sad.

Sometimes I feel worried and sometimes I feel scared.

And just like me, Jess has these kinds of feelings too.

But no matter what...and no matter where...

I love Jess and Jess loves me.

? When do you feel happy?   When do you feel scared?

When do you feel sad?   When do you feel angry?

When do you feel worried?   Who makes you feel loved?

Ben is like me in SO many ways.

He has hopes and dreams of things to come, and so do I!

Jess respects my choice to do whatever I want to do, and be whatever I want to be.

And I respect her choice to do whatever she wants to do, and be whatever she wants to be.

Ben can make choices, and so can I.

We both CHOOSE to treat each other with kindness and respect.

? *What choices do you make?*

Ben is a boy and I am a girl...

but in so many BIG ways...

there is NO difference between us!

Discussion Questions
for Parents, Caregivers, and Educators

Our differences make us unique but it is our 'sameness' that makes us all human. As a society, we often forget our human commonality and see only the differences, when in 'fundamentals' there is no difference between us.

The message in this book is for children to understand from the earliest of years that there are more similarities between people than there are differences. We may be a different gender or from a different culture but we have a human 'commonality'. We all have hopes and dreams, we all have feelings, and we all have the right to make choices. No gender is more powerful or 'better' than another. All genders need to respect our 'sameness' but at the same time respect our choices, which make us unique!

I recommend after discussing each double-page spread and the questions below, that the reader ends with these two summarizing questions, **'What is the same about Jess and Ben? What is different?'** *Note:* sometimes there will be nothing that is different between the children (except what they may be wearing and their physical appearance). I also recommend using pages 6 and 7 to list all the similarities and differences on a T-chart. That is, list all the similarities your child can think of, e.g. both children have eyes, fingers, fingernails, etc. I recommend you do this only the once, as writing the same list for every page will be too much for both of you! The point to this exercise is for children to realize that there is much more the 'same' about the genders than there is different. It is human nature to overlook similarities and search for differences. We tend to categorise things by their differences given their similarities are too numerous to mention. In regards to gender, we simply make the division 'boy' and 'girl' based on people's obvious physical differences rather than note all the other physical similarities, e.g. we all have arms, legs, fingers, etc. The categories of 'boy' and 'girl' are convenient labels in social situations but unfortunately come pre-loaded with assumptions and stereotyping. This book's aim is to break both.

Note: the questions on the internal pages have not been included below.

PAGES 4–5 *Same: both children eat breakfast. Difference: Jess has oatmeal; Ben has eggs on toast.*
Ask, 'Why do you think the author said that Ben and his twin sister are different in "tiny little" ways? What is the "big" way that they are the same? *That's right! Both children eat breakfast!* What do you have for breakfast? What does your sister/brother/mother/father/friend have for breakfast? What is the same about Jess and Ben? What is different?'

PAGES 6–7 *Same: both children have hair. Difference: Ben has short hair. Jess has long hair.*

Ask, 'What is the same about the people in the picture? What choices have the people in the picture made? Could Ben have long hair? Why do you say that? Could Jess have short hair? Why do you say that? Describe how you look. How do you look different from your sister/brother/friend? What is the same about Jess and Ben? What is different?'

PAGES 8–9 *Same: both children enjoy fun activities. Difference: each child enjoys a different kind of fun activity.*

Ask, 'Is it okay for children to like different activities? Why do you say that? What things do you like to do?'

Are they the same activities as your sister/brother/friend? Can girls and boys do the same activities? Why do you say that? What kinds of toys do you like to play with? Are boys' and girls' toys different or the same? Why do you say that? What is the same about Jess and Ben? What is different?'

PAGES 10–11 *Same: both children are maths champs. Difference: none.*

Ask, 'Can girls and boys both be maths/science/spelling champs? Why do you say that? How do you think their teacher is feeling? What is the same about Jess and Ben? What is different?'

PAGES 12–13 *Same: both children play soccer, run fast, like hiking. Difference: none.*

Ask, 'How are the children "equal" in these pictures? What does the word "equal" mean? What is the same about Jess and Ben? What is different?'

PAGES 14–15 *Same: both children enjoy playing doctors with dolls. Difference: none.*

Ask, 'What are the children doing? Do you like to play doctors? Why/Why not? What games do you like to play with dolls? Should both boys and girls play with dolls? Why do you say that? What is the same about Jess and Ben? What is different?'

PAGES 16–17 *Same: both children have hopes and dreams for their future. Difference: they each have different/unique hopes and dreams.*

Ask, 'Why do you think Ben and Jess want to be different things when they grow up? Do you have hopes and dreams of what you would like to be when you grow up? What are they? Is it okay for people to have lots of different types of jobs? Why do you say that? What is the same about Jess and Ben? What is different?'

PAGES 18–19 *Same: both children want to have families when they grow up. Difference: they each wish for different family groupings.*

Ask, 'Do you think both boys and girls want families when they grow up? Why do you say that? What is the same about Jess and Ben? What is different?'

PAGES 20–21 *Same: both children enjoy cooking, reading, and swimming. Difference: Jess likes to cook cakes, read comics, and swim in the sea; Ben likes to cook pancakes, read adventure stories, and swim in a pool.*

Ask, 'Do you think being different in tiny little ways from each other is okay? Why do you say that?

What is something that you and your brother/sister/friend like to do that is the same in a big way but it is different in a tiny way? For example, do you both like flowers? But maybe you like different kinds of flowers. What is the same about Jess and Ben in a big way? What is different in a tiny way?'

PAGES 22–23 *Same: both children have feelings. Difference: none.*

Ask, 'Do girls and boys have the same kinds of feelings? Why do you say that? Can boys/girls feel sad? Can girls/boys feel angry? Can you explain a little bit more about what you mean? What is the same about Jess and Ben? What is different?'

PAGES 24–25 *Same: both children have feelings and feel love. Difference: none.*

Ask, 'Do you think it is okay to tell someone you love them? Why do you say that? What is the same about Jess and Ben? What is different?'

PAGES 26–27 *Same: both children have hopes and dreams for the future, and both children respect each other's choices in life. Difference: none.*

Ask, 'What do you think Jess/Ben is thinking about? What does the word "respect" mean? Why does Ben/Jess have a choice to be whatever they want to be? Why do Ben/Jess need to respect each other's choices? Why is it important that Ben and Jess treat each other with kindness and respect? Do people choose how they treat each other? Why do you say that? What is the same about Jess and Ben? What is different?'

PAGES 28–29 *Same: both are human. Difference: Jess is a girl and Ben is a boy.*

Ask, 'What does it mean that even though "Ben is a boy and Jess is a girl . . . in so many BIG ways . . . there is NO difference between them"? What is the same about Jess and Ben? What is different? How should we treat each other? Does it matter if you are a boy or girl? Why do you say that?'

TRY THIS! After each question on the internal pages, have the child you are reading the book to ask you the same question. Discuss what is the same and what is different about you both.

Books by the Same Author

Some Secrets Should Never Be Kept
'Some Secrets Should Never Be Kept' is an award-winning and beautifully illustrated children's book that sensitively broaches the subject of inappropriate touch. This book was written as a tool to help parents, caregivers, and teachers broach the subject with children in an age-appropriate and non-threatening way. Suitable for children 3 to 11 years.

No Means No!
'No Means No!' is a children's picture book about an empowered little girl who has a very strong and clear voice in all issues, especially those relating to her body. This book teaches children about personal boundaries, respect, and consent; empowering kids by respecting their choices and their right to say, 'No!' Suitable for children 2 to 9 years.

My Body! What I Say Goes!
A book to empower and teach children about personal body safety, feelings, safe and unsafe touch, private parts, secrets and surprises, consent, and respectful relationships. Suitable for children 3 to 9 years.

Pearl Fairweather, Pirate Captain
Captain Pearl Fairweather is a brave, fair, and strong pirate captain. She and her diverse crew of twenty-four women sail the seven seas on the good ship, *Harmony*. All is well, until the day Captain Sandy McCross sails into their lives and demands to take over Pearl's ship! This beautifully illustrated children's book sets out to empower young girls to be strong, assertive, self-confident, and self-reliant, and for boys to respect that empowerment, and to embrace and value it. Suitable for children 5 to 12 years.

Body Safety Education:
A parents' guide to protecting kids from sexual abuse
This essential and easy-to-read guide contains simple, practical, and age-appropriate ideas on how parents, caregivers, and educators can protect children from sexual abuse — ensuring they grow up as assertive and confident teenagers and adults.